We're Very Good Friends, My Uncle and I

Written and Illustrated
by

P.K. Hallinan

For Uncle Mike

CP CHILDRENS PRESS®

CHICAGO

Library of Congress Cataloging-in-Publication Data

Hallinan, P. K.
  My uncle and I.

  (We're very good friends)
  Summary: A boy describes the zany good times he
has with his uncle, who brightens his life and lightens
his days.
  [1. Uncles—Fiction. 2. Stories in rhyme.]
I. Title. II. Series.
PZ8.3.H15My 1989   [E]   89-17264
ISBN 0-516-03650-5   CIP
                                              AC

We're very good friends,
my uncle and I.

We like to sing songs...

and laugh till we cry.

And sometimes we'll stand
in a canyon and shout,
and listen to echoes
go bouncing about.

Or sometimes we'll lie
in a field of tall grass
and make up some game,
like "Catch A Sky Pass!"

We do lots of great things,
my uncle and I.

We splash in the ocean.

We run in slow motion.

We draw in the sand
with our suntanning lotion.

We even make costumes
and funny disguises
to give folks some laughs
or at least some surprises.

And sometimes we'll wrestle
like two wild bears ...

and race up the stairs
like hounds chasing hares.

Or sometimes we'll cruise
in his used Zoommobile...

or chirp back at birds
so they'll know how it feels.

But then we'll tell stories,
the scarier the better,
like "The Rats from New York!"
or "The Mummy's Blue Sweater!"

Then my uncle just winds up
and pours out a yarn
that stretches from here
to the end of your arm.

And once in a while
he'll take an odd stance
and make up a polka
or some crazy dance ...

23

and off we go hopping
and bopping around
like two floppy mops
till we drop to the ground.

We're terrible dancers,
my uncle and I.

But always we're happy
just spending our time
like peas in a pod
and two of a kind.

And if he starts teasing
that I've vanished in air,
and looks high and low
though I'm standing right there...

I don't ever worry
'cause he ALWAYS knows when
to stop his pretending
and hug me again.

Yes, he makes me feel special
in his own special ways.
He brightens my life...

and he lightens my days.

So I guess you can see
there's no secret to why...

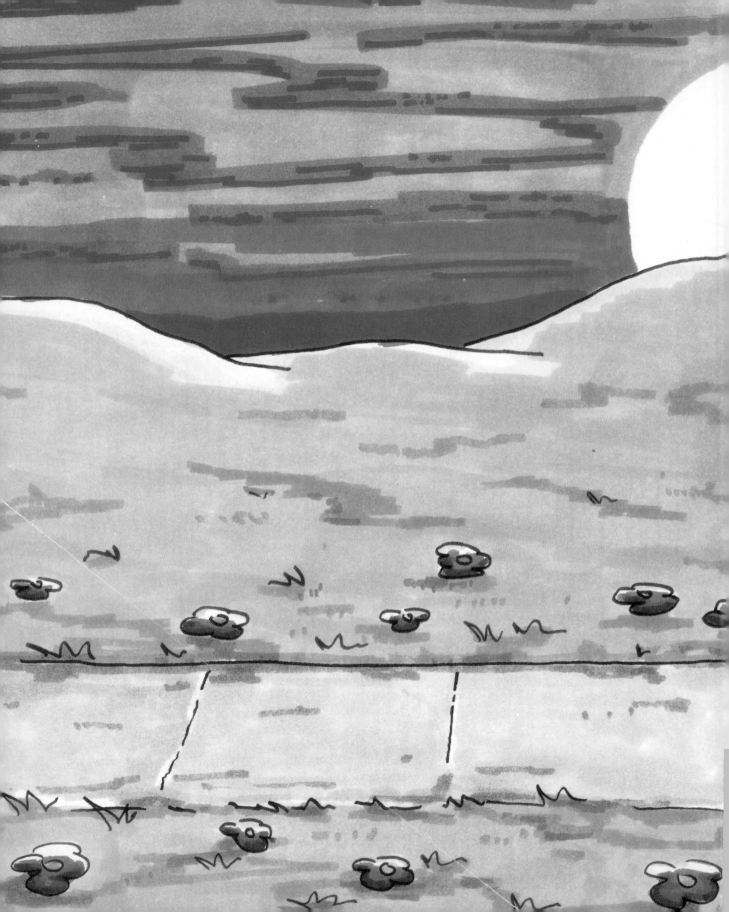

ABOUT P. K. HALLINAN

Patrick Hallinan began writing children's books at the request of his wife who asked him to create an original Christmas gift for their two young sons. Today, nearly twenty years later, P. K. Hallinan is one of America's foremost authors of children's books that teach personal values and self-awareness. His sensitive text and heartwarming illustrations offer a celebration of life to all who visit his very special world.

The little character who appears throughout Mr. Hallinan's books is "P. K.", a blend of his two real-life sons, Kenneth and Michael. Although "P. K." has taken on his own personality over the years, Mr. Hallinan feels that he represents "all children, young and old, who see the world through the eyes of innocence."

Mr. Hallinan lives with his wife, Jeanne, and their three dogs in southern California.